GOSCINNY AND UDERZO

PRESENT

An Asterix Adventure

ASTERIX
AND THE
GREAT DIVIDE

Written and Illustrated by ALBERT UDERZO

Translated by Anthea Bell *and* Derek Hockridge

Asterix titles available now

Original edition © 1980 Les Éditions Albert René / Goscinny-Uderzo
English translation © 1981 Les Éditions Albert René / Goscinny-Uderzo
Original title: *Le Grand Fossé*

Exclusive licensee: Orion Publishing Group
Translators: Anthea Bell and Derek Hockridge
Typography: Bryony Newhouse

The right of René Goscinny and Albert Uderzo to be identified as the authors of this work
has been asserted by them in accordance with the Copyright, Designs and Patents Act 1988.

This revised edition first published in 2004 by Orion Books Ltd,
Orion House, 5 Upper St Martin's Lane, London WC2H 9EA
An Hachette UK company

5 7 9 10 8 6

Printed in China

www.asterix.com
www.orionbooks.co.uk

A CIP record for this book is available from the British Library

ISBN 978-0-7528-4712-2 (cased)
ISBN 978-0-7528-4773-3 (paperback)
ISBN 978-1-4440-1332-0 (ebook)

The Orion Publishing Group's policy is to use papers that are natural, renewable and recyclable products
and made from wood grown in sustainable forests. The logging and manufacturing processes are
expected to conform to the environmental regulations of the country of origin.

GAULISH VILLAGE

COMPENDIUM

LAUDANUM

AQUARIUM

TOTORUM

ARMORICA

BELGICA

LUTETIA

SPQR

GAUL
(ROMAN CONQUEST)
50 BC

CELTICA

AQUITANIA

PROVINCIA

THE YEAR IS 50 BC. GAUL IS ENTIRELY OCCUPIED BY THE
ROMANS. WELL, NOT ENTIRELY ... ONE SMALL VILLAGE OF
INDOMITABLE GAULS STILL HOLDS OUT AGAINST THE INVADERS.
AND LIFE IS NOT EASY FOR THE ROMAN LEGIONARIES WHO
GARRISON THE FORTIFIED CAMPS OF TOTORUM, AQUARIUM,
LAUDANUM AND COMPENDIUM ...

ASTERIX, THE HERO OF THESE ADVENTURES. A SHREWD, CUNNING LITTLE WARRIOR, ALL PERILOUS MISSIONS ARE IMMEDIATELY ENTRUSTED TO HIM. ASTERIX GETS HIS SUPERHUMAN STRENGTH FROM THE MAGIC POTION BREWED BY THE DRUID GETAFIX . . .

OBELIX, ASTERIX'S INSEPARABLE FRIEND. A MENHIR DELIVERY MAN BY TRADE, ADDICTED TO WILD BOAR. OBELIX IS ALWAYS READY TO DROP EVERYTHING AND GO OFF ON A NEW ADVENTURE WITH ASTERIX – SO LONG AS THERE'S WILD BOAR TO EAT, AND PLENTY OF FIGHTING. HIS CONSTANT COMPANION IS DOGMATIX, THE ONLY KNOWN CANINE ECOLOGIST, WHO HOWLS WITH DESPAIR WHEN A TREE IS CUT DOWN.

GETAFIX, THE VENERABLE VILLAGE DRUID, GATHERS MISTLETOE AND BREWS MAGIC POTIONS. HIS SPECIALITY IS THE POTION WHICH GIVES THE DRINKER SUPERHUMAN STRENGTH. BUT GETAFIX ALSO HAS OTHER RECIPES UP HIS SLEEVE . . .

CACOFONIX, THE BARD. OPINION IS DIVIDED AS TO HIS MUSICAL GIFTS. CACOFONIX THINKS HE'S A GENIUS. EVERY-ONE ELSE THINKS HE'S UNSPEAKABLE. BUT SO LONG AS HE DOESN'T SPEAK, LET ALONE SING, EVERYBODY LIKES HIM . . .

FINALLY, VITALSTATISTIX, THE CHIEF OF THE TRIBE. MAJESTIC, BRAVE AND HOT-TEMPERED, THE OLD WARRIOR IS RESPECTED BY HIS MEN AND FEARED BY HIS ENEMIES. VITALSTATISTIX HIMSELF HAS ONLY ONE FEAR, HE IS AFRAID THE SKY MAY FALL ON HIS HEAD TOMORROW. BUT AS HE ALWAYS SAYS, TOMORROW NEVER COMES.

SOMEWHERE IN GAUL, PEACE WOULD BE REIGNING IN A LITTLE VILLAGE VERY LIKE THE VILLAGE WHERE ASTERIX LIVES...

...BUT FOR VARIOUS PECULIAR INCIDENTS. A BIG DITCH HAS BEEN DUG THROUGH THE MIDDLE OF THE VILLAGE, SO THAT NO ONE CAN GET FROM THE RIGHT SIDE TO THE LEFT SIDE.

CLEVERDIX

HAS BEEN ELECTED CHIEF BY THE LEFT OF THE VILLAGE...

NEVER MIND WHAT THE OTHER LOT SAY, I'VE BEEN UNANIMOUSLY ELECTED VILLAGE CHIEF!

MAJESTIX

HAS BEEN ELECTED CHIEF BY THE RIGHT OF THE VILLAGE... MONARCH OF HALF HE SURVEYS.

BY DIVINE RIGHT!

VARIOUS ATTEMPTS HAVE BEEN MADE TO DEAL WITH THE SITUATION...

AND THE VILLAGERS OF THE LEFT AND THE RIGHT ARE EVER READY TO EXPRESS THEIR MUTUAL ANTAGONISM.

RSPRR! RSPRRR!

BUT IT WOULD TAKE POSITIVELY SINISTER DEXTERITY TO SOLVE CERTAIN VITAL PROBLEMS...

?!

?!

...AND ONLY THE CHILDREN ARE ANY BETTER OFF FOR THE RIFT.

SCRUNCH

YOU'VE GOT NO RIGHT TO DO THAT! THAT'S MY TREE!!!

SOME OF THE VILLAGERS, HAVING OPTED FOR NEUTRALITY, FIND THAT IT HAS ITS DISADVANTAGES.

DINNER'S READY!

COMING, DARLING!

BONK!

IN CHIEF CLEVERDIX'S HUT...

LOOK HERE, FATHER, THIS CAN'T GO ON! THAT DITCH DIVIDING US IS A DISGRACE TO THE VILLAGE!

IS THAT MY FAULT, HISTRIONIX, MY BOY? THAT TRAITOR MAJESTIX SANK TO BRIBING SOME OF THE VOTERS!

HE AND HIS HENCHMAN, THE UNSPEAKABLE CODFIX, HAD THE NERVE TO GET VOTES FROM VILLAGERS WHO WERE ONLY BABES IN ARMS!

WELL, AT THIS RATE FUTURE GENERATIONS OF GAULS AREN'T GOING TO THINK MUCH OF THEIR ANCESTORS!

CAN YOU SUGGEST ANYTHING, FATHER?

YES, MY BOY, I CAN. I'VE DECIDED TO MAKE A SPEECH TO THE VILLAGERS OPPOSITE. THAT'LL BRIDGE THE GAP. THEY'LL SOON SEE HOW WRONG THEY WERE TO DITCH ME!

AND IN CHIEF MAJESTIX'S HUT...

OH, FATHER, DO YOU REMEMBER HOW HAPPY THE VILLAGE WAS WHEN WE ONLY HAD ONE CHIEF, ALTRUISTIX?

YES, I DO! THE OLD SO-AND-SO TOOK AFTER HIS COUSIN ALCAPONIX... MAKING OFF WITH ALL THE VILLAGE'S TAXES!

3A

THIS IS ALL THAT FOOL CLEVERDIX'S FAULT! HE STOLE VOTES WHICH WERE MINE BY RIGHT.

HE EVEN PROMISED TO BRING DOWN INFLATION, AND THOSE IDIOTS FELL FOR IT! THAT WAS WHEN THE BALLOON WENT UP!

MELODRAMA IS RIGHT! WE NEED A SINGLE CHIEF TO LEAD THE VILLAGE. YOU LET THEM KNOW OVER ON THE LEFT THAT YOU'RE THE RIGHTFUL CHIEF!

CODFIX, YOUR ADVICE ISN'T ALWAYS CODSWALLOP! YES, I'LL ADDRESS THEM!

AND SOON AFTERWARDS...

3B

7

BROTHERS, WE ARE HOVERING ON THE BRINK OF VILLAGE DISASTER! BUT THE PARTY OF THE LEFT OFFERS FULL EMPLOYMENT... MAXIMUM PRODUCTIVE POTENTIAL FOR ALL WORKERS...

...SHIELDBEARERS INCLUDED. DON'T YOU LISTEN TO MAJESTIX! HE'D PLUCK THE VERY WINGS FROM YOUR HELMETS! WORKERS OF THE VILLAGE, UNITE!

CROSS THE GREAT DIVIDE!

SPLATCH!

POPULAR OPINION HAS REPLIED IN THE ONLY FITTING WAY TO THE LYING INSINUATIONS OF THAT DOUBLE-DEALING CLEVERDIX! WITH HIS BRINKMANSHIP, HE'D HAPPILY SACRIFICE THE GOOD OF THE VILLAGE TO THE INTERESTS OF ROME, SPOUTING HOT AIR ON BEHALF OF THE ROMAN GEEZER*...

* JULIUS CAESAR

FRIENDS, GAULS, COUNTRYMEN, LET US THROW IN OUR LOT TOGETHER!

COME TO MY...

SPLATCH!

VERY WELL, LET'S FIGHT IT OUT, YOU ROTTEN LOT, AND WE'LL SEE WHO'S LEFT IN COMMAND!

BY ALL MEANS, AND WE'LL SEE YOU DO A RIGHT ABOUT TURN!

RSPRRRR! RSPRRR!

9

ELSEWHERE, PEACE IS REIGNING IN ANOTHER LITTLE VILLAGE, A VILLAGE WE ALL KNOW WELL...

LOOK, IF PEACE IS REIGNING IN OUR LITTLE VILLAGE, THE VILLAGE THEY ALL KNOW WELL, THAT MEANS THE ROMANS ARE SULKING, ASTERIX!

NO, OBELIX, IT JUST MEANS THEY'VE LEARNT A BIT OF SENSE!

?!

WHAT ARE YOU DOING ON THAT CONTRAPTION, O CHIEF VITALSTATISTIX?

ER... WELL... I'M GOING OUT SHOPPING FOR IMPEDIMENTA. SHE'S FEELING A BIT UNDER THE WEATHER.

BUT WHAT'S THE CART FOR?

OH, THE CART! THAT'S A NEW IDEA OF MINE. IT MEANS THESE CLUMSY GREAT OAFS CAN'T LET ME DOWN ANY MORE WHEN THE FANCY TAKES THEM.

RIGHT, YOU TWO! WHATEVER YOU DO NOW, I STAND FIRM ON MY TRUSTY SHIELD! SO OFF WE GO SHOPPING!

!

BONG!

SIGH

AND HE CAN'T SHOP US FOR THAT, OR GET NEW SHIELDBEARERS...

NO, WE SHIELD-BEARERS OPERATE A CLOSED SHOP!

DOWNCAST AGAIN, PIGGYWIGGY? THINKING YOURSELF SO CLEVER... HUH! PIGS MIGHT FLY!

10

DINNER'S READY!

DINNER'S READY!

DINNER'S READY!

DINNER'S READY!

DINNER'S READY!

DINNER'S READY!

DINNER'S READY!

DINNER'S READY!

LISTEN, WHY DON'T WE CARRY ON LATER TO HELP OUR DINNER DOWN?

AND MEANWHILE, WOULD YOU MIND HELPING ME DOWN? MY WIFE'S WAITING!

THESE FISH ARE ALMOST PAST IT, EVEN FOR HELPING PEOPLE RELAX. CHANGE AND DECAY IN ALL AROUND I SEE...

13

NIGHT HAS FALLEN, AND ALL IS CALM AGAIN IN THE VILLAGE.

TIME FOR BED, SCHIZOPHRENIX!

COMING, DARLING!

BONG!

CODFIX IS GOING TO ASK THE ROMANS TO HELP MAKE MY FATHER CHIEF OF THE WHOLE VILLAGE... AND IN RETURN MY FATHER HAS PROMISED HIM MY HAND IN MARRIAGE!

HOW DARE HE?! BUT I'M FROM THE OPPOSITE CAMP, MELODRAMA... WHY ARE YOU TELLING ME ALL THIS?

BECAUSE YOU'RE THE ONLY PERSON WITH ANY SENSE IN THIS CRAZY VILLAGE, AND I DON'T WANT TO MARRY CODFIX! O HISTRIONIX, HISTRIONIX! WHERE-FORE ART THOU HISTRIONIX?

?

!?!

RAISE THE ALARM!

BONK!

ARE YOU HURT, HISTRIONIX?

NO, I'M ALL RIGHT... I FANCY A PASSING SHOAL OF FISH BROKE MY FALL!

14

IY OWN DAUGHTER IN LEAGUE WITH THE ENEMY! TREACHERY UNDER MY OWN ROOF!

AND MY OWN FATHER ISN'T ASHAMED TO ASK THE ROMANS FOR HELP IN FIGHTING OUR OWN FRIENDS AND RELATIONS!

SHUT UP, YOU UNGRATEFUL CHILD! I'M GOING TO LOCK YOU IN YOUR ROOM, AND YOU DON'T COME OUT UNTIL THE DAY YOU MARRY CODFIX!

I NEVER WILL! I'D RATHER BE A VIRGIN SERVING VESTA* ALL MY LIFE!

*GIRLS CURRIED FAVOUR WITH THIS GODDESS

DON'T LET'S RUSH THIS MAJESTIX! TIME AND PATIENCE WILL ACHIEVE MORE THAN RAGE AND VIOLENCE EVER COULD!

GNGNGNGN

SOMETIMES I WONDER HOW I THINK THESE THINGS UP...

O LOVELY MELODRAMA, PLEASE ACCEPT THIS PRETTY BUNCH OF FLOWERS!

WHAT MAKES YOU THINK YOU'RE A SMASH HIT WITH ME?

BANG!

11ª

EANWHILE...

FATHER, WAKE UP!

HMPH? WHAT IS IT?

MAJESTIX AND HIS HENCHMAN CODFIX ARE PLANNING TO ASK THE ROMANS TO HELP THEM CONQUER THE WHOLE VILLAGE!

OH, ARE THEY? WELL, SON, I WANT YOU TO GO IN SEARCH OF MY OLD COMRADE-IN-ARMS VITALSTATISTIX. HE AND I FOUGHT TOGETHER AT GERGOVIA...

HE'S CHIEF OF AN ARMORICAN VILLAGE A FEW DAYS' JOURNEY AWAY. THANKS TO THE DRUID GETAFIX'S MAGIC POTION, HE HAS KEPT THE WHOLE MIGHT OF CAESAR'S LEGIONS AT BAY! EXPLAIN IT ALL TO HIM, AND TELL HIM I NEED HIS HELP!

15

A FEW DAYS LATER...

HOW I ENVY THE PEOPLE OF THIS VILLAGE! LIVING IN SUCH PERFECT PEACE AND HARMONY...

SPLATCH

YOU STUPID IGNORANT LOT! I'M NOT SELLING ANY MORE OF MY FISH TO THOSE WHO DON'T APPRECIATE ITS TRUE WORTH!

GOOD!!! THOSE WHO APPRECIATE ITS TRUE WORTH WILL TURN IT INTO GLUE, AND IT WON'T SMELL SO BAD!!!

?!

IF THIS CARRIES ON MUCH LONGER, ASTERIX, THEY'LL BE DISCOVERING NUCLEAR FISHION!

AHEM!

CAN YOU TELL ME WHERE TO FIND VITALSTATISTIX, CHIEF OF THIS VILLAGE?

?

VITALSTATISTIX? HE'S ON HIS WAY!

STOP! AND THAT'S AN ORDER!

SCREECH

I'M GOING TO CRACK UP... I CAN FEEL IT COMING ON! YES... I'M GOING TO CRACK UP...

THIS IS IT! I'M CRACKING UP!

...AND THAT, O CHIEF VITAL-STATISTIX, IS THE SAD STORY OF OUR VILLAGE. ONLY YOUR DRUID GETAFIX'S MAGIC POTION AND THE WISDOM OF YOUR EXPERIENCED WARRIORS CAN SAVE US!

HMPH, YES. SPEAKING OF THE WISDOM OF MY EXPERIENCED WARRIORS, I SOMEHOW FEEL I SHOULD BE PUTTING MY OWN HOUSE IN ORDER FIRST...

...BUT SINCE THE ROMANS LOOK LIKE GETTING MIXED UP IN YOUR AFFAIRS, I DON'T SEE WHY I SHOULDN'T LEND MY OLD COMRADE-IN-ARMS CLEVERDIX A HAND!

THANK YOU... AND ON MY OWN BEHALF TOO! UNLESS WE FIND A PEACEFUL SOLUTION, MELODRAMA AND I CAN NEVER HOPE TO BE UNITED!

BOOHOOHOOO

?

BOOHOOHOOHOO

WHAT'S THE MATTER, OBELIX?

SNIFF! I GET ALL UPSET BY LOVE STORIES WITH UNHAPPY ENDINGS! SNIFF!

HUH!

BUT THIS STORY'S ONLY JUST BEGINNING, AND IF CHIEF VITALSTATISTIX WILL LET US, WE'RE GOING TO HELP HISTRIONIX SOLVE HIS PROBLEMS!

OOH, YES, LET'S! GOODY, GOODY, GOODY!

WOOF! WOOF!

THE ROMANS AROUND HERE ARE KEEPING VERY QUIET JUST NOW, SO I THINK I CAN JOIN THE EXPEDITION MYSELF! THE PEOPLE OF YOUR VILLAGE MAY NEED ME TO HELP THEM BRIDGE THE GREAT DIVIDE!

...AND A LITTLE LATER...

WILL HE SING? WON'T HE SING? WILL HE SING? WON'T HE SING?

IN THE ROMAN CAMP NEAR THE DIVIDED VILLAGE...

HEY, SOURPUS, I'LL SWAP YOU TWO SENTRY DUTIES FOR ONE LAUNDRY FATIGUE!

NOTHING DOING! YOU ALREADY OWE ME THREE COOK-HOUSE FATIGUES AND TWO LATRINE FATIGUES!

BACK AT THE RECRUITMENT OFFICE, THEY TOLD US WE'D GET BEAUTIFUL SLAVE-GIRLS FROM THE COUNTRIES WE CONQUERED...

BACK IN ROME, CAESAR SAID HE WAS COUNTING ON US TO CLEAN UP THE BARBARIANS... WHAT A WASH-OUT!

LOOT, THEY SAID. THE CARROT FOR THE DONKEY!

IT'S A MAN'S LIFE IN THE ARMY, THEY SAID...

ALL RIGHT, WE KNOW, WE KNOW

DECURION INFECTIUS VIRUS, THIS TENT IS A PIGSTY, AND THE COOKING IN THE CAMP IS GOING FROM BAD TO WORSE!

I KNOW. THE COOKHOUSE IS REVOLTING, O CENTURION UMBRAGEOUS CUMULO-NIMBUS. THERE'S A MOOD OF GENERAL UNREST. THE MEN WANT SLAVES TO DO THE DIRTY WORK, BUT CAESAR SAID WE WEREN'T TO TAKE SLAVES DURING THE ROMAN PEACE!

WISH I'D BROUGHT MY SLAVEGIRL FROM HOME... NICE LITTLE ROMAN PIECE* SHE IS!

*PAX ROMANA

CENTURION, I HAVE THE ANSWER TO ALL YOUR PROBLEMS!

?!

WHO LET YOU INTO THIS CAMP, GAUL?

THE MAN ON DUTY AT THE GATE. HE WAS QUITE HAPPY WHEN I OFFERED HIM A SLAVE IN EXCHANGE!

WHO ARE YOU, ANYWAY? HOW DARE YOU CORRUPT MY LEGIONARIES?

I'M FROM MAJESTIX, RIGHTFUL CHIEF OF THE RIGHT SIDE OF OUR VILLAGE. I'M HIS ALTER EGO AND RIGHT HAND!

TAP, TAP!

AND THIS IS MY LEFT FOOT! BE OFF, OR IT'LL ALTER **YOUR** EGO!

CHIEF MAJESTIX WANTS YOU TO HELP HIM PUT DOWN A REBELLION LED BY CLEVERDIX!

THAT'S NONE OF MY BUSINESS! THIS IS YOUR NUNC DIMITTIS... **GET OUT**, OR YOU'LL BE SINGING A DIFFERENT TUNE. A FUNERAL DIRGE FROM HYMNS ANCIENT*!

*HYMNS MODERN AS YET UNWRITTEN

WHY, YOUR VILLAGE LOOKS MORE PEACEFUL THAN OURS!

YES, I DON'T WANT TO CRY STINKING FISH, BUT THE AIR CERTAINLY SEEMS CLEARER HERE!

DON'T YOU BELIEVE IT. THERE'S A SLUMBERING VOLCANO UNDER THOSE THATCHED ROOFS... ONE WHICH COULD ERUPT INTO VIOLENCE AT ANY MOMENT!

??? RSPRRR!

TAP! TAP! TAP!

I KNEW I COULD COUNT ON MY OLD FRIEND VITALSTATISTIX! YOUR MAGIC POTION WILL STOP THAT OAF MAJESTIX IN HIS TRACKS!

LET'S GET THINGS CLEAR RIGHT AWAY, CLEVERDIX...

I DOLE OUT MAGIC POTION ONLY FOR FIGHTING ROMANS, NEVER FOR USE IN QUARRELS BETWEEN GAULS!

BUT WHAT CAN WE DO IF MAJESTIX AND HIS WARRIORS ARE FIGHTING SIDE BY SIDE WITH THE ROMANS?

THINGS HAVEN'T COME TO THAT YET, AND WHILE WE'RE WAITING FOR THE ROMANS TO COME...

THE ROMANS ARE COMING! THE ROMANS ARE COMING!!!

16

21

YOU KNOW, FATHER, MAJESTIX REALLY DID ACT IN A MANNER WORTHY OF A CHIEF!

ALL THINGS CONSIDERED, I MUST ADMIT HE CARRIED IT OFF IN STYLE!

WE'LL GET THEM THIS TIME, ASTERIX!!!

NO, OBELIX! IT COULD PUT MAJESTIX AND HIS WARRIORS IN DANGER!

A LITTLE LATER...

DON'T WORRY, MELODRAMA! IF MY FATHER WILL AGREE, WE'LL ORGANIZE A CAMPAIGN AGAINST THE ROMANS TO FREE OUR FELLOW VILLAGERS!

WE MUST DO SOMETHING, HISTRIONIX!

SNIFF!

HUH!

I CERTAINLY AGREE! MAJESTIX MAY BE MY OPPONENT, BUT I DON'T WANT HIM USING HIS SACRIFICE AS AN ARGUMENT AT THE POLLS!

WAIT A MOMENT! I'VE GOT A BETTER IDEA!

THE ROMANS OF THESE PARTS DON'T KNOW GETAFIX, OBELIX AND ME. WE'LL GO TO THE ROMAN CAMP ON OUR OWN, IF IT'S SLAVES THEY WANT, WE'LL APPLY FOR THE JOB, AND SET THE PRISONERS FREE!

AN EXCELLENT IDEA, ASTERIX!

OOH, YES! GOODY, GOODY, GOODY! A CHANCE TO SAMPLE THE LOCAL ROMANS AT LAST...

CLAP! CLAP! CLAP!

... THUMPING ROMANS IS LIKE HAVING DINNER: IT'S NICE TO EAT OUT FOR A CHANGE!

THE ROMAN
MP...

WE WILL NEVER BE YOUR SLAVES, ROMAN!

DO YOU KNOW THE PENALTIES FOR A SLAVES' REVOLT? YOU'D BETTER STOP AND THINK, UNLESS YOU WANT TO MAKE THE LIONS IN THE CIRCUS MAXIMUS AT ROME A SQUARE MEAL!

AND WHILE THEY'RE THINKING, CHAIN THEM ALL UP WELL!!!

CAN I HAVE THOSE THREE SENTRY DUTIES BACK? THE ONES YOU SWAPPED FOR MY COOKHOUSE FATIGUE!

PRICES HAVE RISEN... IT'LL BE FOUR SENTRY DUTIES NOW!

MEANWHILE...

GOOD LUCK, FRIENDS!

DON'T WORRY, MELODRAMA! THANKS TO GETAFIX'S KNOW-HOW, OBELIX'S STRENGTH, DOGMATIX'S NOSE AND MY CUNNING, WE'LL SOON HAVE YOUR FATHER HOME!

FUNNY HOW SURE OF THEMSELVES CLEVERDIX'S ALLIES SEEM! I'LL FOLLOW THEM AT A SAFE DISTANCE!

DOGMATIX HAS BEEN SNIFFING ABOUT EVER SINCE WE LEFT! I THINK HE'S PICKED UP THE SCENT OF A BOAR!

NO, NO, IT'S JUST A RED HERRING.

IF SO, IT'S BEEN TAKING CODLIVER OIL!

SNIFF! SNIFF!

RIGHT, YOU GET THE IDEA, OBELIX? WE'RE HUMBLE SLAVES, SO NO THUMPING THE ROMANS!

LISTEN, ASTERIX...

...IS THERE SUCH A THING AS A SLAVE-DOG?

23

HALT! WHO GOES THERE, AND WHAT DO YOU WANT?

GAULISH SLAVES, AND WE WANT TO SERVE THE ROMAN ARMY!

THAT'S A BIT OF LUCK! WE'VE JUST GOT SOME BRAND-NEW SLAVES IN, BUT THEY WON'T SERVE YET!

AND I'LL KEEP THIS FAT SLAVE FOR MYSELF!

BONK!

I MAY BE A SLAVE, BUT I AM NOT FAT!

TAP! TAP! TAP!

WELL, JUST HOW DO YOU EXPECT THEM TO TAKE US SERIOUSLY NOW, OBELIX?

I THINK I CAN FIX IT...

THIS FLASK CONTAINS AN ELIXIR OF MY OWN INVENTION! A FEW DROPS WILL INSTANTLY RESTORE THIS ROMAN TO FULL HEALTH AND STRENGTH...

AND HE WON'T EVEN REMEMBER WHAT HAPPENED!

HALT! WHO GOES THERE, AND WHAT DO YOU WANT?

GAULISH SLAVES, AND WE WANT TO SERVE THE ROMAN ARMY!

HERE WE GO AGAIN...

AMAZING! THOSE GAULS ARE AMAZING. AND I CAN'T HELP WONDERING WHAT TRICK THEY'RE PLANNING TO PLAY ON THE ROMANS!

AND I'LL KEEP THIS FA...

NO! DON'T!

SO SORRY, WE'RE CLASS 1 SLAVES, AND WE CAN'T SERVE THE RANK AND FILE!

?!?

HOW DID HE GUESS WHAT I WAS GOING TO SAY?

THE DRUID FORGOT HIS FLASK! I ABSOLUTELY MUST GET HOLD OF IT. IT COULD COME IN USEFUL!

ALWAYS THE SAME OLD STORY! THE RANK AND FILE DON'T HAVE ANY RIGHT TO...

CLANG!

NOW TO OBSERVE DEVELOPMENTS DISCREETLY! I FIND THESE GAULS MORE AND MORE INTRIGUING!

THREE NEW GAULS HAVE JUST ARRIVED, CUMULONIMBUS! THEY WANT TO BE YOUR SLAVES.

?!? I SHALL CERTAINLY NEVER UNDERSTAND THE GAULS!

O ROMAN, I AND MY FRIENDS HAVE COME TO OFFER YOU OUR CULINARY SKILLS! NAME YOUR DISH, AND I CAN COOK IT TO PERFECTION. JUST ORDER THE MENU, AND SEE WHAT HAPPENS!

26

GLUG GLUG GLUG

GLUG GLUG GLUG

NO, OBELIX, NOT YOU!

AND WHY NOT HIM?

YES, WHY NOT ME?

BECAUSE HE FELL INTO THE CAULDRON WHEN HE WAS A BABY, AND... ER... UM...

AND HE HAS TO STAY ON A STRICT DIET FOR THE GOOD OF HIS MENTAL HEALTH, THAT'S WHY NOT HIM!

DON'T WORRY, WE'RE HERE TO RESCUE YOU. THE POTION WILL GIVE YOU THE STRENGTH YOU NEED. WATCH FOR OUR SIGNAL! THEN YOU HAVE NOTHING TO LOSE BUT YOUR CHAINS!

?!

SOON AFTERWARDS...

YOU SEE, ROMAN, THERE WAS NO NEED FOR YOU TO WORRY!

WELL, SINCE THERE ISN'T ANY SOUP LEFT, LET'S GO STRAIGHT ON TO THE NEXT COURSE ON THE MENU, WHICH IS...

THE CHOP! PAF!

THE MENU! I SEE IT ALL NOW!!!

SO DO WE! COME ON, MEN!

SNAP!

IT WAS ALL BECAUSE OF THAT DREADFUL CODFIX!

YES, AND WHERE'S THE TWO-TIMING SO-AND-SO NOW?

HE DISAPPEARED WHEN YOU LEFT.

HUH! HE'LL BE LOOKING PRETTY GREEN AROUND THE GILLS WHEN I FIND HIM!

YOU KNOW, I FEEL CODFIX MAY STILL BE FISHING IN THESE TROUBLED WATERS!

YES. WE DON'T WANT HIM TURNING THE SCALES...

OUR OWN QUARREL ISN'T SETTLED YET, YOU KNOW, YOU ROTTEN OLD FRAUD!

IT CERTAINLY ISN'T! AND THIS TIME IT'LL BE A FAIR FIGHT, YOU ROTTEN OLD OPPORTUNIST!

YES, WELL, MEANWHILE YOU'D BETTER BARRICADE YOURSELVES INSIDE THE VILLAGE, IN CASE THE ROMANS DECIDE TO COME BACK!

AND I'M GOING TO BREW UP SOME MAGIC POTION... ONLY TO BE TAKEN IF THE ROMANS DO COME BACK, OF COURSE!

JUST AT THAT MOMENT, HOWEVER, THE ROMANS HAVE NOT RECOVERED FROM THEIR LITTLE SETBACK. MEANWHILE...

NOW THAT THE WHOLE VILLAGE IS AGAINST ME, I'D BETTER MAKE USE OF THE ROMANS TO SATISFY MY THIRST FOR VENGEANCE...

...AND A FEW DROPS OF THE DRUID'S ELIXIR, ADDED TO THIS WINE, WILL HELP ME WHEN THE CENTURION COMES TO SATISFY HIS THIRST!

SOUND THE ASSEMBLY!

RIGHT! WE SHALL NOW FORGET THIS WHOLE UNFORTUNATE EPISODE AND CLEAR UP THE MESS! I WANT THE GARRISON ALL SPRUCED UP AND LOOKING LIKE A CENA CANIS*! DISMISS!

* LATIN: DOG'S DINNER

WHAT'S CENA CANIS?

DOG LATIN, YOU IDIOT!

AH, A NICE GOBLET OF WINE WILL HELP ME FORGET MY TROUBLES!

GLUG! GLUG! GLUG!

AAAAAH! BY JUPITER, I'M FEELING ON TOP OF THE WORLD!

27A

?!? WHO ARE YOU, GAUL, AND WHO LET YOU INTO THIS CAMP?

IT'S WORKING!

I'VE COME TO WARN YOU, O CENTURION! THE GAULS OF THE NEARBY VILLAGE HAVE BROKEN THE PAX ROMANA! THEY'VE BASHED UP YOUR LEGIONARIES AND RANSACKED YOUR CAMP!

IMPOSSIBLE! OR ARE YOU GIVING ME SOME INSIDE DOPE?

O CUMULONIMBUS, THE MEN DON'T WANT TO CLEAR UP THE MESS! THEY'RE ALL REPORTING SICK!

SICK BAY

27B

32

AND LATER...

I STILL HAVE NO IDEA WHO YOU ARE, GAUL, BUT YOU WON'T FIND ME UNGRATEFUL FOR SERVICES RENDERED!

WE CAN TALK ABOUT THAT LATER, ONCE YOU'VE DONE FOR THE VILLAGE AND ALL ITS INHABITANTS.

BUT WATCH OUT! THERE'S A DRUID WITH THEM, AND HE HAS A POTION WHICH MAKES ANYONE WHO DRINKS IT INVINCIBLE!

CENTURION, A COUSIN OF MINE STATIONED IN ARMORICA TOLD ME ABOUT A DRUID THERE WHO HAS STRANGE POWERS, AND I'M JUST WONDERING WHETHER...

YOU'VE GOT A POINT, INFECTIUS VIRUS! WE MUST BE CAREFUL!

MEANWHILE, IN THE GAULISH VILLAGE...

THE MAGIC POTION'S READY. WE'D BETTER PUT IT SAFE ON NEUTRAL GROUND SOMEWHERE WHILE WE WAIT TO SEE IF THE ROMANS ARE COMING BACK!

SCHIZOPHRENIX'S HUT IS NEUTRAL GROUND. IT'S BANG IN THE MIDDLE OF THE VILLAGE.

YES, LET'S PUT IT THERE. THAT FOOL SCHIZOPHRENIX HAS NEVER BEEN ABLE TO DECIDE WHICH SIDE HE'S ON!

DIDN'T YOU EVER THINK OF PUTTING FLOOR-BOARDS DOWN OVER THE GAP?

THAT'S FLOORED HIM! WE'LL DO IT NOW.

'D SO, A 'TTLE LATER...

I'LL WATCH OVER THE CAULDRON TONIGHT, TO MAKE DOUBLY SURE!

THEN YOU'D BETTER HAVE THIS GOURD OF MAGIC POTION, ASTERIX. YOU NEVER KNOW, YOU MIGHT NEED A BOOSTER DOSE, IN SPITE OF THE POTION IN THE CAULDRON.

AND THAT NIGHT, ON THE OUTSKIRTS OF THE WOOD NEAR THE GAULISH VILLAGE...

I DON'T TRUST THAT DRUID AND HIS SECRET WEAPONS! I THINK I'D BETTER GO SCOUTING AHEAD BEFORE WE ATTACK!

AND WHATEVER YOU DO, DON'T MOVE TILL I GET BACK!

RIGHT, BUT HURRY UP! I CAN'T WAIT TO GET MY REVENGE ON THOSE GAULS!

THE GODS OF THE UNDERWORLD ARE ON MY SIDE! IT'S THAT FOOL CONGENITALIDIOTIX ON SENTRY DUTY! I'LL SOON DEAL WITH HIM!

HALT! WHO GOES THERE?

IT'S ME. CODFIX.

I MIGHT HAVE KNOWN FROM THE SMELL! WHAT DO YOU WANT?

I WANT TO ASK CHIEF MAJESTIX TO FORGIVE ME!

YOU CAN COME IN, BUT IF I WERE YOU I'D KEEP MY DISTANCE FROM MAJESTIX!

WHY ARE YOU MOUNTING GUARD LIKE THIS? WHAT ARE YOU AFRAID OF?

WE'RE AFRAID THE ROMANS MAY COME BACK. BUT LUCKILY GETAFIX THE DRUID HAS MADE US SOME OF HIS MAGIC POTION. IT'S SAFE IN SCHIZOPHRENIX'S HUT!

TEEHEE!

I'VE NEVER BEEN ABLE TO SEE STARS INSIDE A HUT BEFORE!

BONG!

I'M SURE I SHALL NEED SOME OF THIS!

I FEEL QUITE SORRY FOR CODFIX, APOLOGIZING TO THE CHIEF... HE MUST BE HAVING TO STEEL HIMSELF WONDER IF HE'LL GET AWAY WITH IT?

?!

CRAAASH!

HELP! HELP!

DO SOMETHING, GETAFIX! GIVE HIM SOME OF THE ELIXIR YOU USED ON THE ROMANS!

I'M SORRY, MY DEAR OBELIX, I'M AFRAID I MUST HAVE LEFT IT NEAR THE ROMAN CAMP!

ANYWAY, IT WOULD BE DANGEROUS TO GIVE IT TO ASTERIX. ANYONE WHO DRINKS MY ELIXIR CAN'T TAKE THE MAGIC POTION AFTERWARDS... THE MIXTURE HAS SOME RATHER STRANGE EFFECTS!

BUT LUCKILY ASTERIX IS ALL RIGHT!

THIS TIME I REALLY DO THINK THE SKY HAS FALLEN ON MY HEAD!

THE SKY'S FALLEN ON EVERYONE'S HEAD, ASTERIX! CODFIX HAS STOLEN THE MAGIC POTION, AND HE'S SURE TO DOSE THE ROMANS WITH IT.

HUH! MAGIC POTION OR NO MAGIC POTION, WE CAN DEAL WITH THE ROMANS!

SPOKEN LIKE THE TRUE SON OF A CHIEF!

HMPH!

THE SUN'S COMING UP! YOU TOOK YOUR TIME, GAUL! I THOUGHT YOU WERE PLANNING TO BETRAY US!

BETRAY YOU? LOOK WHAT I'VE GOT HERE! **THE MAGIC POTION WHICH MAKES ANYONE WHO DRINKS IT INVINCIBLE!**

ARE YOU SURE IT'S...

WATCH THIS!

CRAAACK!

! ! ! ! ! !

CLAP CLAP CLAP CLAP CLAP CLAP CLAP CLAP CLAP CLA

32

NEVER MIND THE CURTAIN CALLS! IT'LL BE CURTAINS FOR US IF WE DON'T GET ON WITH DRINKING IT!

SOON AFTERWARDS...

THAT'S IT! EVERYONE'S HAD HIS POTION. COMING TO JOIN THE ATTACK?

ER... NO... NO, IT WOULD BE BETTER FOR ME NOT TO BE SEEN WITH YOU! IT'S A MATTER OF PRINCIPLE, YOU KNOW!

FORWARD MARCH!

I MAY STILL JUST HAVE TIME TO BREW UP SOME MORE PO...

THE ROMANS ARE COMING!

WE MUST GO OUT TO MEET THE ROMANS AND FIGHT THEM, IF WE'RE TO SAVE THE VILLAGE!

33

36

THESE ROMANS ARE REALLY CRAZY THEY'RE NOT AT THE CIRCUS NOW!

AND MEANWHILE...

BING!

BANG!

BONG!

AHA! NO MORE GLOBE-TROTTING! WE'RE BACK TO NORMAL!

PICK UP YOUR WEAPONS AND GET BACK TO BATTLE STATIONS!!!

35A

O CUMULONIMBUS, I'M AN OLD SOLDIER, AND I'VE BEEN AROUND, BUT I'VE NEVER FOUGHT IN TERRAIN QUITE LIKE THIS!

I'LL TELL YOU ANOTHER FUNNY THING... WE'VE LOST SIGHT OF THE ENEMY!

BUT WE'RE STILL HERE, O ROMAN!

?!?

EEEEK!

35B

GIANTS! THEY'RE GIANTS!

NO, WE AREN'T! YOU'RE THE ONES WHO'VE SHRUNK! IN FUTURE YOU'LL KNOW BETTER THAN TO TAKE MAGIC POTION WITHOUT A DRUID'S PRESCRIPTION!

GOT AN INFERIORITY COMPLEX DOWN THERE? YOU'D BETTER SEE A SHRINK!

MERCY! BY ALL THE GODS, MAKE THIS NIGHTMARE STOP!

YOU'LL SOON BE BACK TO YOUR NORMAL SIZE, BUT FIRST YOU MUST SWEAR TO LEAVE THE VILLAGE AND ITS PEOPLE IN PEACE!

I SWEAR! MAY I FADE AWAY IF I BREAK MY OATH!

OFF YOU GO BACK TO CAMP, ROMANS, AND MIND WE NEVER FIND YOU IN THIS NEIGHBOURHOOD AGAIN!

NOW HURRY UP AND GET OUT, BEFORE DOGMATIX DECIDES YOU'D MAKE A TASTY MORSEL OR SO!

GRRRRRRRR...

HA HA! HA HA HA! HA HA HA!

WOOF! WOOF!

40

42

MEANWHILE...

SUNK IN SALT WATER... SUNK IN FRESH WATER... ALL THE WATER I EVER WANT AGAIN IS A NIP OF AQUA VITAE!

YOU'RE GETTING THE LINGO NICELY... YES, IT'S TERRA FIRMA FOR ME, TOO.

QUICK, LET'S GO AND SET MAJESTIX'S MIND AT REST!

IN TIMES OF TROUBLE SUCH AS THIS, IT IS ONLY RIGHT TO FORGET OUR DIFFERENCES, AND I FEEL FOR YOU, MAJESTIX!

THEY'RE BACK, WITH MELODRAMA!

OH FATHER, HISTRIONIX ACTED LIKE A TRUE CHIEF!

I'M EXTREMELY GRATEFUL TO HISTRIONIX FOR HIS BRAVE ACTION, BUT THAT'S GOING A BIT TOO FAR, MY DEAR!

OH NO, IT ISN'T. AFTER ALL, HISTRIONIX IS THE SON OF A CHIEF!

SON OF A CHIEF MY FOOT!!! I'M THE ONLY REAL CHIEF AROUND HERE!

OH, FOR GOODNESS' SAKE, WE'VE HAD ENOUGH OF THIS! IF YOU MUST FIGHT FOR THE CHIEFTAINSHIP KEEP IT BETWEEN THE TWO OF YOU!!!

?!

?!

MELODRAMA IS QUITE RIGHT! FIGHT IF YOU MUST, BUT LEAVE THE OTHER VILLAGERS OUT OF IT. THEY'VE HAD ENOUGH OF YOUR QUARRELS!

AND SOON AFTERWARDS...

NOW, YOU SENILE OLD DOTARD, I'LL SHOW YOU WHAT A REAL CHIEF CAN DO, AND WITH MY BARE HANDS!

YOU DYSPEPTIC OLD FOGY! YOU'RE IN FOR A SHOCK!

44

YOU'LL NEED A NEUTRAL UMPIRE. I VOLUNTEER TO REFEREE YOUR SINGLE COMBAT!

ACCORDING TO THE RULES, THE FIGHT MAY GO ON UNTIL SUNRISE TOMORROW. THE LOSER IS THE MAN WHO STAYS DOWN AFTER A COUNT OF 100! OFF YOU GO, AND MAY THE BEST MAN WIN THE PRIZE!

BONK!

CLONK!

V SESTERTII ON CLEVERDIX!

XV ON CLEVERDIX!

X ON MAJESTIX!

41A

EVENING COMES ON, MANY OF THE AUDIENCE, ...RING OF THE SHOW, LEAVE THE RING

PAF!

PAF!

THEY OUGHT TO REVISE THE RULES OF THESE PRIZEFIGHTS.

IT'S LATE. I'M GOING TO BED, ASTERIX!

YAAAWN! SO ARE WE, DOGMATIX AND I DON'T TAKE MUCH INTEREST IN FIGHTS WHEN THERE AREN'T ANY ROMANS OR ANY BOARS.

ZZZZZ

...EN ASTERIX IS UNABLE ...KEEP HIS EYES OPEN. ...ALONE, IN THE MOON-...HT, THE TWO CHIEFS ...E STILL EQUALLY MATCHED

PAF! PAF!

BZZZZ!

AND AT SUNRISE...

COCKADOODLE-DO!

?!?

RRRR! ZZZZ!

41B

FRIENDS, FATE HAS DECIDED THE RESULT OF THE SINGLE COMBAT... NO ONE HAS WON AND NO ONE HAS LOST!

BUT YOU CAN HAVE A YOUNG, STRONG CHIEF IF YOU CHOOSE HISTRIONIX TO LEAD YOU, AND MELODRAMA WILL MAKE A WISE AND BEAUTIFUL CHIEF'S WIFE!

HURRAH! LONG LIVE HISTRIONIX! LONG LIVE MELODRAMA!

?!?

OH WELL, I RATHER THINK ALL WE CAN DO IS GET DRESSED AGAIN!

YOU SAID IT, FAT-FACE!

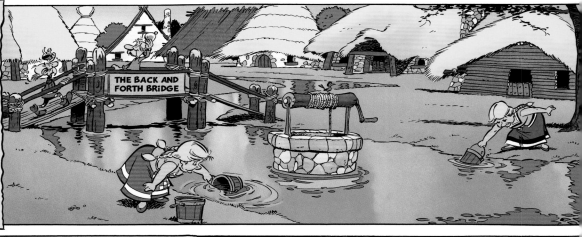

REUNITED AT LAST, UNDER THE RULE OF THEIR NEW CHIEF HISTRIONIX, THE GAULS OF THE VILLAGE DIVERT PART OF THE NEARBY RIVER INTO THE DITCH, WHICH NO LONGER SERVES ANY USEFUL PURPOSE. AND NOW THERE IS NO PARTY OF THE RIGHT OR PARTY OF THE LEFT, ONLY A RIGHT BANK AND A LEFT BANK, RUNNING WATER ON EVERYONE'S DOOR-STEP AND FREEDOM FOR ALL THE VILLAGERS TO GO TO AND FRO.

THE BACK AND FORTH BRIDGE

THE CHILDREN CAN STILL GATHER THE FRUITS OF OTHER PEOPLE'S LABOURS WITH IMPUNITY...

SCRUNCH!

YOU'VE GOT NO RIGHT TO DO THAT! THAT'S MY TREE!!!

NEW AND PRACTICAL USE IS FOUND [FO]R THE TWO GATEWAYS OF THE VILLAGE. [HE]RE YOU SEE THE FIRST ONE-WAY [SY]STEM KNOWN TO ANCIENT HISTORY.

AND SCHIZOPHRENIX'S HUT IS REBUILT AT LAST... THOUGH THE ARCHITECTS DID SLIP UP HERE AND THERE IN THEIR PLANS.

SPLOSH!?

ANY IDEA WHAT BECAME OF THAT SCOUNDREL CODFIX?

NO, BUT I SHOULD BE SURPRISED IF HE WAS STILL UP TO DIRTY WORK.

SURE ENOUGH, IN THE ROMAN CAMP...

WELL, SLAVE, HAVE YOU DONE THOSE VEGETABLES YET?

AND THE LAUNDRY? AND DON'T FORGET THE IRONING!

[TH]E WEDDING OF MELODRAMA AND HISTRIONIX [IS] CELEBRATED AMIDST REJOICINGS FOR ALL [AN]D BOARS FOR SOME.

SCRUNCH! SCRUNCH

SCRUNCH! SCRUNCH

[THE] TIME [CO]MES TO SAY [GO]ODBYE.

HOW CAN WE EVER THANK YOU FOR ALL WE OWE YOU?

YOU'RE HAPPY, AND THAT'S ALL THE THANKS WE NEED!

HUH!

47

THE END

48